Last–But–Not–Least

Last-But-Not-Least

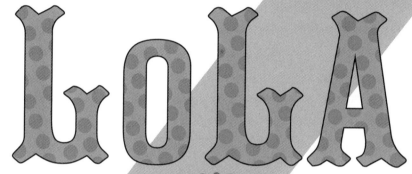

LOLA

AND THE
CUPCAKE
QUEENS

Christine Pakkala PICTURES BY Paul Hoppe

BOYDS MILLS PRESS
AN IMPRINT OF HIGHLIGHTS
Honesdale, Pennsylvania

Boyds Mills Press
An Imprint of Highlights
815 Church Street
Honesdale, Pennsylvania 18431

Printed in the United States of America
ISBN: 978-1-62091-596-7 (hc) • 978-1-62979-694-9 (pb) • 978-1-62979-433-4 (e-book)
Library of Congress Control Number: 2015936721
First paperback edition, 2016
The text of this book is set in ITC Novarese Std.
The drawings are done in pen on paper, with digital shading.
10 9 8 7 6 5 4 3 2 1

For my sister, Kathy, with love
—CP

For Maria & Gerhard
—PH

CONTENTS

1. STINKMANDA AND FUSSY

MY NAME IS LOLA ZUCKERMAN,

and Zuckerman means I'm always last. Just like zippers, zoom, and zebras. Last. Zilch, zeroes, and zombies.

ZZZZZZZ when you're too tired to stay awake. *ZZZZZZZ* when a bee is about to sting you. Z. Ding-dong LAST in the alphabet.

That's a problem when your teacher is in love with the alphabet. Tomorrow at school, we're going to share all about our Halloween costumes. By the time Mrs. D. gets to me, nobody will be listening. I could say, "I'm going to be a stick of butter," or, "I think I'll be a lump of dough." Amanda and Jessie will be playing Miss Mary Mack. Harvey will be hanging off his chair. Savannah will be daydreaming. That's when you're wide awake but you're not paying a bit of attention.

Mrs. D. says we have to be problem solvers. And when she says "we" to me, she means *me*. But I'm lying here in my bed draining my brain battery out and I can't think of a single good solution.

There's a crack in my wall shaped like a "C." If my name was Lola Cool or Lola Cracker Jack or even Lola Drool, I'd be right near the front of the alphabet. Everyone would be listening up to hear all about my Halloween costume.

"LOLA!" my brother Jack hollers.

"WHA-AT?" I yell.

I whip open my door and *YAAAAAGH!*

Something white jumps out at me.

I take a flying leap back and smack onto my bed.
"*AAAGH!*" I scream.

Then I take a second look.

It's just an old sheet.

With an old smelly brother underneath it.

Patches comes running into the room, barking
his head off. He jumps onto the bed with me.

"I AM THE GHOST OF ZUCKERMAN MANSION!"
Jack calls in his old-scary-movie voice.

I leap up and whip the sheet off him.

Jack falls on the floor laughing.

"Not funny!" I yell. I sling a pillow right at his not-ghost face.

"Your friends are here," Jack says. "Stinkmanda and Fussy."

"What's going on up there?" Mom calls.

"Nothing, Mom," Jack says. "I just did what you told me."

"Well, come on, Lola!" she hollers. "Amanda and Jessie are waiting for you in the kitchen."

I hop off my bed. "Just wait until I tell Mom," I say.

"Oh, really?" Jack says in a squeaker voice. "Did I scare the widdle baby?"

"I'm not a baby."

"*HUNH!*" He jumps at me.

"*ACK!*" I jump back. Then I hurry down the hall. I keep looking over my shoulder to make sure Jack stays put.

"Hi, Lola!" Amanda says.

"What was all that hollering about?" Jessie asks.

"Jack stubbed his toe." 'Cause I'm not a widdle baby.

Mom gives us some carrots and hummus to snack on, then goes into her sewing room. She's making a brand-new batch of Lola dresses for those people out in California.

Jack zooms into the kitchen. "Oh, look at the cute little kids."

"We're not little kids," I inform him.

Jack pauses above me. "Lola, when was the last time you brushed your hair?" He pokes at my head.

"Stop poking me, you fake-ghost poker!"

Jack pokes me again.

"Is it okay if we take our snack outside?" Amanda asks politely.

"Yeah, let's get away from your brother," Jessie says.

We head into the backyard and sit in a pile of leaves. Patches lays his head on Jessie's lap.

"You don't get any privacy at your house, do you?" Jessie asks. She pats Patches on the head.

"No," I say. "Patches, get off!" But Patches doesn't move. "He likes you!"

"My dog used to be best friends with Patches," Amanda says.

"Now your dog is best friends with my brand-new, super-deluxe, purebred dog," Jessie says. I get a sour feeling in my stomach, like I ate a whole jar full of dill pickles.

"Well, la-di-da," I say. "Patches has a new best friend, too."

"Who?" they both ask.

"Savannah's dog," I say.

"I didn't know she had a dog," Amanda says. She frowns. That's when you fold up your forehead. Principal McCoy's face got stuck that way. "What's its name?"

I take a deep breath. "Um . . . Jessie."

"Wait a second. Her dog has the same name as me?" Jessie says. "I don't believe you!"

"It's true," I yelp. I hold up a giant yellow leaf and cover my face with it like it's a mask. Only it doesn't cover the whole thing. I can still see Jessie.

"Who's taking care of Jessie-the-dog while Savannah's visiting Old Sturbridge Village?" Jessie asks.

"Er . . . I am," I say.

"Well, where is she?" Jessie asks. She squints at me with laser vision to see if I'm lying.

I get a real sad look on my face. "Jessie ran away. Far away."

"Really?" Amanda sticks out her little finger. "Pinkie-promise?"

"Pinkie-promise," I squeak. "Mom and I put up LOST DOG signs everywhere."

"I guess she's not lying," Jessie says. But Amanda's pinkie is squeezing tight on mine.

"Have you told Savannah yet?" she asks.

"Not yet. I have to go over to her house tonight when she gets home. Or I'll tell her tomorrow at school," I add on.

"She's going to be really mad at you," Jessie says.

"No, she won't," I explain. "'Cause we're getting her a brand-new dog!"

Amanda folds her arms across her chest. "Really, Lola?"

"Well . . ." I say, "maybe. If we can't find Jessie."

"You should get her a puppy," Amanda says. "A fluffy little golden retriever."

"Or maybe I'll rescue a dog from the animal shelter," I say.

Amanda claps her hands. "Oh, that's a really good idea!"

"Never mind that," Jessie says. "Look what I've got." She whips a catalog out of a big pocket in her Lola dress. She unfolds it and holds it up.

"World's Deluxe Costumes," I read off the cover. "Wow!" I'm not *that* excited, but anything's better than talking about Jessie, the Dog That Ran Away (Fingers Crossed) or The New Puppy I'm Getting Savannah (Fingers Crossed Part Two).

Jessie opens up to the center of the catalog.

"Ooh," we three say. Because there they are: The Cupcake Queens. Vanilla Sprinkles, Chocolate Cherry, and Strawberry Sweetie Pie. They have their own TV show, their own book, and their own action figures.

"There's one for each of us," Jessie says.

I look a little closer at the Cupcake Queen costumes. They cost A LOT. I bet Mom and Dad will say no. I told Mom I wanted to be Zero for Halloween because Zero is last and I feel sorry for it. But Mom is too busy running her sewing machine

day and night. *Rrrrr. Rrrr.* And go make yourself a snack because you're a big girl.

"And guess what?" Jessie announces TV-style. "My mom did the advertising for World's Deluxe Costumes, so they let her take a bunch of super fantastic costumes! Including the Cupcake Queen costumes!"

We jump up and Patches rolls in the leaves. We yell, "OOGA BOOGA! OOGA! BOOGA! We're the Cupcake Queens!"

Even if that *Cupcake Queens* show is kind of bo-oring.

"But what about Savannah?" Amanda asks. "Won't she be sad?"

"Not with a new puppy," Jessie says.

"Yeah, right," I agree, but quiet. Because I wish we could stop talking about the Pretend New Puppy.

"And what about your mom?" Amanda asks. "She always makes you a great costume every year."

"Not this year," I say, and "this" stands for all those kids in California who want Lola dresses.

Whooooooooooo. WHOOOOOOOOOOOO.

The three of us freeze.

"Did you hear that?" I ask.

"Was it Patches?" Amanda whispers.

We look at Patches. He looks back at us and wags his tail.

I peer into the house. Peering is a cross between peeking and fearing.

Mom's inside the kitchen, holding up a big hula hoop. I can just barely see Jack, in his room upstairs.

Whoooooooooooo. WHOOOOOOOOOOOOOO.

If it's not Mom and it's not Jack, what is it?

1½. GUH-GUH-GUH GHOST

DAD PULLS MY COVERS TO MY chin.

"Can you tell me a story, Dad?"

Dad has loads of stories and my Uncle Charlie is in every single one. I call Uncle Charlie "Chuncle" 'cause I couldn't say "Uncle Charlie" when I was a little kid.

Guess what? When I have sleepovers at Chuncle's apartment in New York City, he tells bedtime stories. And my dad is in every single one.

Dad says, "One time when Uncle Charlie and I were about your age, Grandma drove us out to Smitty's Family Farm on Long Island to pick a pumpkin for Halloween.

Well, Grandma was talking to someone and it seemed like it was taking forever to get started. So Uncle Charlie and I decided to head off on our own. We saw one great pumpkin after another. Before we knew it, we were lost. Everywhere we looked, we saw pumpkins."

"How lost?" But I have a secret. I've already heard this story, 'cause Chuncle told me.

"Really, really lost. All we could see were pumpkins, and Uncle Charlie started to cry."

"Chuncle said you were the one who cried," I tell him.

"No, it was Chuncle, all right," Dad says.

"He said it was you."

"Well, maybe it was both of us. And it was a good thing we cried so loud, because Grandma found us."

"You were really scared, weren't you?"

"We were," Dad says. "But Grandma was never very far away. We didn't need to be afraid."

Dad kisses me good-night and tells me Mom is going to come in and say good-night in one second.

"But you've got to wait for Mom," I remind him. "In case of ghosts." Even though Mom said ghosts aren't real and all that screaming that we did upset Mrs. McCracken next door who was trying to enjoy her patio on a nice fall evening. And Mrs. McCracken is always feeling soupy and low and our screaming just about gave her a heart throb.

After one hundred and thirty-nine seconds and

more 'cause I lost count, Mom comes in. I close my eyes to pretend I'm asleep 'cause it took Mom so long to get in here.

"She's asleep," Mom whispers to Dad. "I'm going to finish up the dishes."

I spring open my eyes. "No, I'm not," I say.

Mom sighs and that's not nice.

"Can you tell me a good-night story, Mom?" I ask.

"I'll do the dishes," Dad says. And he kisses me good-night again.

Mom sits on my bed and smooths down my hair, only I bet that didn't work. "Of course, little Lola Lou," she says.

"Can you tell me about the time you had a really

bad fever and you only liked strawberry ice cream?" I ask her.

Jack must have heard. He comes in and cuddles up next to me because we both like this story and we both miss Mom, even though he's never said so. I'm his sister and that's how I know stuff about him that's secret.

"Strawberry ice cream and sliced strawberries and strawberry Jell-O," Mom says.

"Why didn't you love chocolate ice cream?" Jack asks.

"Because I loved strawberry."

"I would have loved chocolate ice cream," Jack says.

"I would have loved Rocky Road," I say.

"Well, I loved strawberry ice cream. And even after I felt better, I asked my mom—"

"Granny Coogan," Jack and I interrupt.

"Yes, I asked Granny Coogan if I could only eat strawberries. So Granny Coogan gave me

strawberries for breakfast, strawberries for lunch, and . . ."

"Strawberries for dinner!"

"And after three days of nothing but strawberries . . ."

"You begged for a grilled cheese!" we yell.

"And I never wanted to see a strawberry again. Well, at least not for a very long time."

"What about now?" Jack says. "Do you love strawberries now?"

"They're not my favorite," Mom says, only I am thinking about strawberry bushes, and inside those bushes there's a cozy pillow and a blanket and . . .

hear *KA-BOOM!* and I sit right up in my bed.

FLASH! Lightning shines in my room. And I see it! A ghost hunkers down in the corner.

I scream and scream and scream and scream.

Mom and Dad come running in and flip on my light.

And that's when I go and sleep in their bed.

2. ONCE UPON A PUPPY

"DOES COFFEE MAKE YOU STAY awake?" I ask Mrs. D. She is busy writing *ONCE UPON A PUMPKIN* on the chalkboard.

Amanda and Jessie just went to the bathroom to brush their hair and fix their bows and headbands. "You should come with us," Jessie said. "Your hair is kind of messy."

"That's how I like it," I told her. And I really hope they stay in there for a good long time. So I can tell Savannah about her new pretend puppy when she gets here. She better come soon. Because if Amanda finds out about my Jessie Dog and New Puppy Fib (okay, Lie), I'm guessing she won't like me anymore, in permanent marker.

"Why, I suppose it does," Mrs. D. says. That gives her a good idea, I guess, and she takes a sip from her travel mug. "And that thunderstorm we had last night."

I give a big yawn. "Then I'm going to start drinking it."

"Why are you tired, Lola?" Mrs. D. asks.

"I had to keep one eye open while I was sleeping," I tell her. "On account of the ghost at my house."

Harvey comes barreling into the room. "Ghosts? That's nothing. I've got a werewolf in my backyard."

Mrs. D. smushes her lips together. "Hmm, I can see we're going to need a little discussion about Halloween myths."

"What's a myth?" Harvey asks.

"A myth is a make-believe story. It's something that gets handed down from generation to generation," Mrs. D. explains.

"So a myth is a lie story," I say.

"Not exactly, Lola. For example, one Halloween myth is that if you dream of a white cat, you will be lucky. It's not exactly a lie, is it? It's more of a wish. And zombies and ghosts are not lies, but fears."

"But I heard it hallooing in my backyard, and later on I woke up and saw it in my bedroom, and my mom and dad said it was just my laundry hamper but I think it was a ghost, so that's why I never wanted to keep both of my eyes shut at the same time," I say. My lip feels a little wobbly, like it wants to bike right off my face.

Amanda and Jessie crowd up next to me. They're brushed back in place.

"We heard it too, Mrs. D.," Jessie says. She shivers.

"It was scary!" Amanda says.

"I'm sure there's a sensible explanation," Mrs. D. says. "Maybe it was the rumbling from the approaching thunderstorm, girls. No need for concern. Did you ask Mom or Dad?"

"Yes. But Mom has too much on her plate right now to go looking for something that's howling and invisible and just some figs in my imagination. And in Amanda's. And Jessie's."

And speaking of those FRIENDS, Amanda and Jessie go to the back of the room to sharpen their pencils. Only they play Miss Mary Mack. Fishsticks. I want to go back there and get in the way. But first I have to tell Savannah about Jessie-the-dog.

I post myself at the door. Where is that Savannah Travers? Where in the ding-a-ling-ring-ding could she be?

Then she comes around the corner with Gwendolyn Swanson-Carmichael and she's got on a Ye Old Cap from Old Sturbridge Village.

"Hi, Savannah!" I holler down the hall. She and

Gwendolyn amble up to our classroom. Amble is when you walk so slow you might as well just sit down. "Savannah, have you ever wanted a puppy?" I ask Savannah when she gets close, but she's too busy talking to Gwendolyn about apple pie recipes from the olden days.

"There's apple-custard pie and cheesy-apple pie and green-apple pie and candy-apple pie and cran-apple pie and apple-meringue pie and caramel-apple pie . . ."

Finally, and that's a really long time so that you could go back to bed and wake up again and you would still have to wait, Savannah is done telling Gwendolyn about all the different apple pies there were in the olden days.

"How about apple cakes?" Gwendolyn asks. She rubs her tummy. "I bet they had some tasty apple cakes."

"Well—" Savannah says.

"Speaking of dogs . . ." I interrupt.

"Huh?" Savannah says.

"Well, how do you feel about dogs?"

Savannah smiles. "I like hot dogs with loads of ketchup and mustard."

"I mean hairy dogs. The kind that bark and jump up on your bed."

"Oh. I like cats. I have a cat named Arthur who we rescued from a shelter. Arthur sleeps on my bed and purrs me right to sleep."

Fishsticks.

"I don't like dogs or cats," Gwendolyn says. "I'm allergic." And she flounces off. Flounce is when you bounce away with flair.

"Wouldn't Arthur

like a puppy friend?" I ask Savannah.

Savannah opens her mouth. But before she can tell me Arthur would LUH-HUV a puppy friend, I see Amanda and Jessie barreling right for us. It's the Miss Mary Mackers Attackers. Uh-oh.

Lickety-spit, I change the subject.

I pat Savannah on the back. "That IS a good-looking pilgrim cap. Maybe you could be a pilgrim lady for Halloween. Isn't that a great idea?"

Savannah shakes her head. "Oh, no. I want to be Strawberry Sweetie Pie, the Cupcake Queen. She's my most absolute favorite."

I feel my mouth plop open. "But . . ."

"And I'm going to ask my mom if I can order the costume after school today, too! I'm going to wear it trick-or-treating. And I'm going to love it because I watch *Cupcake Queens* all the time and I did in California and it's my favorite." Savannah says all those words in one big gasp.

"But—"

"I had a real Strawberry Sweetie Pie cake for my birthday. And one more thing. Last year I got to meet all three Cupcake Queens at Sweet Surprises Play Park."

I stare and stare at Savannah because that's the most words she's ever said in a row.

"How about you, Lola?" Savannah asks. "What do you want to be?"

"Er . . ."

Amanda and Jessie nestle right up to us.

"Poor, poor Savannah," Jessie

says. "Are you mad at Lola? So, so mad?"

"Are you sad?" Amanda asks.

Savannah peers out of her jumbo-sized glasses. "Why would I be mad or sad?"

"Because of Jessie," Jessie says.

"Jessie-the-dog." Amanda helps out.

"Your dog," I explain. "The one I lost and then you had to get a puppy. A really cute puppy."

"Oh," Savannah says. "And did I lose the puppy, too?"

"Nope," I say. "You still have the puppy."

Jessie folds her arms up tight. "Hey, what's that all about? How come you don't know if you have your own puppy or not?"

RING!

"Candy Corns, take your seats," Mrs. D. calls. "We have a LOT to cover today."

"Well?" Jessie leans in close to Savannah. "Is Lola lying?"

"Lola," Amanda says in the most Who-Made-This-

Mess Parent Voice you ever heard, EVER. "You pinkie-promised!"

Savannah looks at me, then at Jessie, then at Amanda.

"GIRLS!" Mrs. D. holler-reminds us.

"I did get a puppy," Savannah zaps out. Then she hurries off to her seat. And guess what color her face is? Liar-Liar-Hot-Sauce-Fire Red.

3. YES, THEY ARE SO REAL GHOSTS

"CLASS!" MRS. D. CALLS. WE keep talking.

Clap, clap, clap-clap-clap. Mrs. D. is trying to get hold of our attention. But even Gwendolyn Swanson-Carmichael is yakking away about her Halloween costume.

TWEET! TWEET! Mrs. D. blasts a whistle. Harvey grabs his ears.

Whoo-whee. We all shut our traps at the exact same moment.

Mrs. D. says, "I know that everyone is VERY

excited about Halloween on Friday."

She smiles and has a dreamy look on her face. I know she's imagining all the candy she's going to get when she goes trick-or-treating. 'Cause she luh-huvs candy.

"Gumdrops, what are some of the things you think of when I say the word 'Halloween'?" Mrs. D. asks.

"Candy!" we shout.

Mrs. D. writes *candy* on the board.

"Pumpkins!"

She writes *pumpkins* on the board, right underneath *candy*.

"Ghosts!" I say.

Now Mrs. D. starts another column on the board and she writes *ghosts*.

"Werewolves," Harvey says.

She writes *werewolves* right under *ghosts*.

We also tell her "witches" and "goblins" and she puts those right under *werewolves*.

Finally, we have two really long columns.

Mrs. D. asks, "Who can tell me what the difference is between these two columns?"

Timo Toivonen shoots up his hand. "In Finland, we do not celebrate Halloween."

"Thank you, Timo. Can you tell me the difference between these two columns?" Mrs. D. has her Waiting-For-Toast-To-Pop-Up look.

"No," Timo says. "They both contain Halloween items. In Finland, we dress up and trick-or-treat on Easter."

"You've got that wrong!" Harvey bursts out. "Easter is for chocolate bunnies."

"I don't celebrate Easter," Ben Wexler says. "I celebrate Passover."

"I celebrate *Día de los Muertos* and Halloween," Jessie says.

Mrs. D. takes a swig of coffee from her travel mug.

Ruby Snow shoots up her hand. "In the first column, it's all stuff to eat."

"What about the black cat?" Gwendolyn Swanson-Carmichael points out. "You can't eat a black cat."

"Unless it's a cookie shaped like a black cat," John Carmine Tabanelli says.

I think I know the answer. I shoot up my hand. "In the second column, that's all the stuff that scares

the living daylights out of you." I smile my I'm-Right Smile at the whole class. "That's the really true stuff about Halloween. The other stuff is just food."

"Actually," Gwendolyn says in her You're-Not-Right Voice, "the first column is things that are real. The second column is things that are made up. Right, Mrs. D.?"

"Yes," Mrs. D. says. "Ghosts and goblins and witches are make-believe." She writes *Make-believe* over that list. She writes *Real* over the other list.

Harvey asks, "What about werewolves?"

"Make-believe, too," Mrs. D. says. "It's nice to

have fun on Halloween with costumes and candy. But it's also nice to remember that it's make-believe."

Humph. Mrs. D. is always right. But I know what I heard last night. And what I saw. It was a spooky, scary, ding-dong dead ghost.

Mrs. D. just called me a ball-face liar, teacher-style.

3½. LOLA PUMPKINMAN

MRS. D. POINTS TO THE CHALK-
board where she wrote *ONCE UPON A PUMPKIN*.
"Lollipops, this is the play we're going to put on for
the Second Grade Play Festival."

"Ooh! Ooh!" Harvey yells. "I want to be the
pumpkin!"

"Harvey," Mrs. D. says, "Hand, please. And
inside voice."

She lifts up a black witchy cauldron from her desk.
"In this cauldron are scraps of paper. On them are

the names of the characters in the play. I'm going to walk around the class, and you will reach into the cauldron and pull out a name. Do NOT unfold your scrap of paper until everyone has one. Also, remember, you get what you get . . ."

"And you don't get upset!" we yell.

One by one, everyone pulls out a piece of paper. "Okay, go ahead and look!" Mrs. D. says.

I read: *The Pumpkin*. Fishsticks. I wish this play was called *Once Upon a Turnip*. 'Cause the pumpkin has got to be the main guy. And I don't want to be the main guy. I raise my hand.

"Do I have to be The Pumpkin?" I ask.

Mrs. D. takes a swig from her travel coffee mug. "Lola, what did I just say?"

Savannah raises her hand, and Mrs. D. gives her The Nod.

"Lola, you should be the pumpkin because you have pumpkin-colored hair," Savannah says.

Somebody in the class snickers. Somebody else laughs. Then somebody else. Pretty soon everyone in the class is laughing.

Everyone but me.

"CLASS!" Mrs. D. bellows. "That will be enough!" Mrs. D. smiles at me with her Butterscotch Smile.

My self is on fire like a mean ol' jack-o'-lantern.

And I am mad mad mad at that Savannah Travers.

"Candy Corns, I'm asking that we memorize our lines by next Wednesday so that we'll be able to perform the play next Friday."

"Friday!" Harvey squawks.

"Yes, a week from Halloween. That way we spread out the fun." Mrs. D. takes a sip from her travel mug. "We will use class time and home time to memorize our lines. Everyone has no more than seven lines. And if you get stuck during the play, I will be right there to help you."

"But that will be REALLY embarrassing," Jessie says without even raising her hand.

And then I have a not-so-good feeling in my stomach like the time Jack talked me into going on the Raging Waters Roller Coaster.

'Cause I remember standing up at my Uncle Charlie's birthday party and all I was supposed to say was a poem. I knew it by my heart. But when I saw all those people, I just forgot every single word. I forgot my uncle's name and I forgot how to take a breath.

It was bad enough at a restaurant in Manhattan with all of Chuncle's friends staring at me.

But it will be a whole lot worse when I can't remember in front of THE WHOLE SCHOOL.

And it's all Savannah Travers's fault. Maybe.

4. I AM RED AND PINK AND A LITTLE BIT GREEN

WE HAVE SPANISH, AND WE learn how to say "Where is the library?" (*¿Dónde está la biblioteca?*) and some other stuff, and Charlie Henderson gets a nosebleed and goes to the nurse. But I have pumpkin on the brain.

Mrs. D. starts talking about Halloween all over again.

"Today we're going to share what we're going to be for Halloween. But instead of telling the class, we're going to describe our costume and the class

49

will guess!" Mrs. D. says. "So take out your writing journals and write a description of your costume without naming what it is."

I take out my watermelon-smelling pencil and my purple notebook.

"Oh, one more thing," Mrs. D. says. "Today we're going from *Z* to *A*. So we'll begin with Lola, and whoever guesses Lola's costume will go next."

Me first? *Z* first! Yay!

But my yay sputters out. *Grrr* sizzles inside me.

Pumpkin hair?

Fishsticks to that.

I write and write and write.

There. That was easy. Maybe. But what about poor ol' Savannah Travers?

Poor ol' pumpkin-caller.

After a while everyone is done scratching away.

"All right, Lola, come on up," Mrs. D. says.

I march up to the front of the class.

"Amanda and I already know what Lola's going to

be for Halloween," Jessie says. "Because my mom is getting her a super-deluxe costume. And one for me and one for Amanda."

"Thank you for sharing that," Mrs. D. says in an I-Mean-The-Opposite Voice. "In that case, you and Amanda should not guess what Lola's costume is."

Poor Amanda gets all red in the face like she did something wrong.

Not Jessie. She says, "Well, fine."

"I infer that Lola, Jessie, and Amanda will be dressed in similar costumes," Jamal Stevenson says.

Jamal uses words like "infer" that you have to guess at to know what they mean.

"Hey, you're not playing the game right," Gwendolyn says. "You have to wait for Lola's description."

"Carry on, Lola," Mrs. D. says. She takes a swig from her travel mug.

I look at all the faces waiting for me to talk. One of them jumps out at me. On account of giant eyeglasses. And behind those giant eyeglasses is a droopy face. My sizzle kind of drizzles.

"I am red and pink and a little bit green. I wear a crown because I rule a yummy world. I can frost a hundred cupcakes in a minute—"

Savannah Travers jumps up and runs right out of the room.

Without even asking permission.

And now my sizzle goes *splat*.

I made Savannah sad.

5. LOLA ZEROMAN

MRS. D. CALLS OUT, "SAVANNAH!"

But Savannah keeps right on going.

"Mrs. D., can I go get her?" I ask. "Please? I'll bring her right back." I put five extra pleases on my face and a beg in my voice.

Mrs. D.'s forehead wrinkles up. Then she nods. I walk out the door and skip-run down the hallway just in time to see Savannah zip into the music room.

But when I look in there, I don't see anybody. I

just hear some huffy-style breathing.

There's a row of music stands and a piano and a whole pile of instruments. But no Savannah. Maybe my eyes trick-or-treated me and it was a trick.

CLANG CLANG!

GACK! I jump straight up in the air!

"Savannah?" My voice comes wobbling out.

Was that a ghost?

"How could you, Lola?" Savannah pops out from behind a tuba. "When I'd just told you that I want to be Strawberry Sweetie Pie. How could you get up in front of that class and tell everyone that YOU'LL be Strawberry Sweetie Pie? That's NO FAIR!"

I stare at Savannah and—fishsticks! That's the second time today she's set a world record for Savannah Travers talking.

"Well, you said I'm a pumpkin-head," I say, but her mad squashes my voice right down to a squeak.

"No, I did not. I said you have that color hair."

"Well, that's not nice."

"I like your hair. My hair is mouse-brown. That's what my Great-Aunt Prudence said."

I look at Savannah's hair. "No, sir. It's brown-sugar brown."

"Brown-sugar brown," she says.

And even though Savannah's face is scrunchy

with sad and mad, she smiles.

"Now I'm going to have to be the great big pumpkin and I don't want to. And I don't really like Strawberry Sweetie Pie, 'cause that show is not my favorite," I say in a ripple like the bunch of papers that got blown off Mrs. D.'s desk when I accidentally turned the fan on. "It's just like Jessie said. Her mom got three fancy costumes and that's what happened."

"But Strawberry Sweetie Pie is my absolute favorite."

"Well . . ." Lola Gooderman is having a fight inside of me with Lola Badderman. And Lola Badderman doesn't want to lose. I never wanted to be a Cupcake Queen in the first place. But now that

Amanda and Jessie are being Cupcake Queens, I want to stick to them like frosting.

"And one more thing," Savannah says in her whispery voice that sounds like a single leaf blowing all by its lonesome self. Then she stops.

"One more thing . . . what?" I ask.

"Well, you told a lie about the dog. And I could have told on you but I never did."

I don't know what to say to that. So I stomp over to a tuba resting all by itself. I put my lips on the tuba and BLOW!

Savannah jumps back. Then she stomps over to a drum set. She picks up the sticks. *WHAM!*

HONK! I blow.

WHAM! She smacks.

The door flies open and bangs on the wall.

Uh-oh. It's Dr. Witherspoon, the music teacher. *BLAM!* She drops a whole box of kazoos right to the floor. And wouldn't you know they go flying everywhere like kazoo airplanes?

"GIRLS!" Dr. Witherspoon belts out—*WASSAH*—just like a karate chop. "What in the WORLD are you doing here in the MUSIC room? Why aren't you in CLASS?"

6. A GLOB OF MUD

SAVANNAH AND I SIT OUTSIDE
Principal McCoy's office. We've been waiting so
long we probably missed Halloween. And maybe
the Second Grade Play Festival. It must be
Thanksgiving already.

"You may now go in," Mrs. Crowley, the secretary,
says.

"You may go first," I tell Savannah.

"No, you may go first," she says.

"Fine," I say. "I'm friends with Principal McCoy
anyway."

He's standing at his door. And guess what? The cast on his arm is off! It's just in a nice soft sling.

"Howdy there, Principal McCoy!" I say, extra-friendly.

"Hello, Lola," he says.

I waltz right in and plunk down in the fuzzy orange cat chair. 'Cause I know Principal McCoy likes me when I'm sorry and I mean it. And I'm always sorry and I always mean it.

But I turn around in the chair to see what's taking Savannah so long to get on in here. And there she is standing in the doorway and her eyes are wetted up and she's chomping on her lip. Principal McCoy is crouching down and talking real soft to her.

I hop out of the cozy chair and hurry on over. "What's wrong with you?" I ask. "Did you stub your toe?"

"N-n-n-no," she cries. "I've just never ever gotten in trouble and gone to the principal's office. I'm not bad like you."

"I'm not bad!" I yell, but part-way through I turn the volume down because yelling is bad. Especially right in front of the principal. "She's the one running out of class and hiding in the music room and getting Dr. Witherspoon to drop a whole box of kazoos on the floor."

"Well, she's the one hogging the best costume and telling whoppers about missing dogs!" Savannah belts out.

"Come sit, girls," Principal McCoy says. "Why don't we all calm down?"

We get settled into two chairs and I let Savannah

have the hard one in case she thinks the fluffy-like-a-cat one has claws like I used to before I sat in it a couple of times.

"Now, who would like to explain how the two of you ended up in the music room blowing and banging on the instruments?" Principal McCoy asks.

"I went in there for some alone time," Savannah says.

"And I went in there to get her back to class," I

say. "Where she left. And I had permission. And she didn't."

"Well, I had strong feelings," Savannah says. "And my mom teaches yoga in a hot room. And she says everybody needs alone time. That gets you processing your feelings."

"I don't get it," I say to Savannah.

"I think Savannah is saying that she was sad," Principal McCoy explains. "Why were you sad?"

Then Savannah tells Principal McCoy ALL about the Cupcake Queens and Strawberry Sweetie Pie.

"Well, girls, this is quite a problem," says Principal McCoy. "How are you going to solve it?"

"We could both be Strawberry Sweetie Pie Cupcake Queens," I say.

Principal McCoy gets a big grin. I get a big grin. Problem solved.

Sniff, sniff.

Savannah's sad all over again.

Principal McCoy's smile slips right off.

"Savannah," Principal McCoy says. "Why don't you tell us why you're upset? Again?"

"I can't," she sniffs.

"Did your mom go back to California?" I ask.

"No," she says. "It's just that I want to be the only Strawberry Sweetie Pie. I don't want there to be two."

"Chances are there will be more than one on Halloween when you trick-or-treat," Principal McCoy says.

"But not in Mrs. D.'s class," Savannah says. "And Lola is already special because she's Z and last."

"That's not special!" I say. "That's just last."

Principal McCoy makes a finger bridge. He thinks for a minute. "Savannah, I can understand why you want to be the only Strawberry Cutie Pie . . ."

"Sweetie Pie," me and Savannah say at the same time. And that makes us both smile.

All of a sudden, Lola Gooderman gives Lola Badderman a surprise karate chop.

"I don't even care about being Strawberry Sweetie Pie," I say really fast. "But Amanda and Jessie wanted me to. So I could match with them and be like the show." *The dumb show*, I think, but I keep it to myself because if you don't have anything nice to say, keep a lid on it. Granny Coogan told me that one. She's got a lid on it almost all the time except when Grampy Coogan let his hound dogs sit on her brand-new sofa and matching loveseat.

And uh-oh. 'Cause Savannah's shiny eyes start

leaking tears all over her freckles.

"But they'd be just as happy if you could be Strawberry Sweetie Pie," I say, as fast as Mrs. McCracken's cat Dwight White zips when Patches is chasing him.

"Oh, Lola!" Savannah says. She springs right out of her chair and wraps her arms around me and gives me a big tight hug. "Oh, thank you! Thank you!"

"I can always be something else," I say. "Like a glob of mud."

And on our way out the door, Principal McCoy says, "Lola, I'm very proud of you. It feels good to make someone else feel happy, doesn't it?"

Fishsticks. 'Cause that's the kind of question adults ask when they already know the answer.

7. GUESS WHO?

ALMOST THE WHOLE CLASS
already played the WHOLE COSTUME GUESSING
GAME. Except for Savannah. And I need a do-over.

"Mrs. D., I'm not going to be Strawberry Sweetie
Pie," I say. "Can I go again?"

Mrs. D. looks at me. Then at Savannah. Then she
nods.

"I'm picking a new costume," I tell everyone.

Amanda's mouth drops open. So does Jessie's.

"I'm round as a circle," I say.

Madison Rogers's hand shoots up. "The sun?"

"Nope. I have a hole in my middle," I say.

Ruby Snow waves her hand. "A donut?" she guesses.

"Nope. I'm three minus three."

"Zero!" Sam Noonan yells. I pretend I don't hear him 'cause teachers don't hear yellers.

Gwendolyn waves her hand in the air. I call on her.

"Zero?" she asks.

"That's right!" I say. "You're next." Only Gwendolyn already went, since almost the whole class played the game without us.

Mrs. D. writes *Lola* at the end of one long column and then *Zero* at the end of another. She luh-huvs columns.

I sit down.

Savannah hurries to the front. "I've got pink legs."

"A flamingo!" Madison guesses.

"I have a pretty dress with a bow."

"Santa!" Rita Rohan guesses.

"I have a strawberry on top of my head."

"Strawberry Sweetie Pie," Amanda calls out. She has a big smile on her face. Fishsticks.

"Yes," Savannah says, only she kind of yells it.

Amanda's up next. I guess she couldn't figure out anyone's costume. Poor, poor Amanda. Even Timo guesses Chocolate Cherry Cupcake Queen.

Timo says, "I am Finnish."

"Are you Timo?" Harvey asks.

"Yes, I am."

"You can't be yourself for Halloween," Harvey says, but not mean.

"Is your Halloween character also Finnish?" Mrs. D. asks.

"Yes. I am the son of Ilmatar."

"In real life or are we guessing your costume?" Rita asks.

"Guessing my costume," Timo says. "Here's another clue. It took 730 years for me to be born."

"Are you Finnish molten lava?" Ben Wexler asks.

Timo shakes his head. "I discovered fire in the belly of a fish in the belly of a fish in the belly of a fish."

We all groan.

"Timo, perhaps you could give us one more clue," Mrs. D. says. "And then you may have to tell us if no one can guess."

"Very well," Timo says. "I will give you a very

good clue. I am the popular folk hero of the Finnish national epic poem *The Kalevala*."

"You're Väinämöinen," Sam shouts. "'Cause you told me at recess yesterday that Väinämöinen is the Finnish Superman.

"Yes!" Timo says with a big smile.

After Timo, there's only Charlie and we all know he's Sir Rodney Strong from Charlie's most absolute favorite book series, Sir Rodney and the Battles of Glockenshnitt.

Mrs. D. stands in front of us. "Now everyone gets to guess who I will be for Halloween," she says. "I love mud."

"Are you a pumpkin seed?" Dilly Chang guesses.

"No, I'm not, but that's a lovely idea," Mrs. D. says. "I travel by crawling," she adds.

"Are you a baby?" Gwendolyn asks.

"No. But you're right, babies do love mud and they do crawl."

"Not me," Harvey says. "My mom said I never crawled. I just started walking."

Mrs. D. says, "That seems believable. Okay, here's another clue. I breathe through my skin."

We're stumped.

"One more. I eat garbage," Mrs. D. says.

"You're a worm!" I yell. "An earthworm!"

"You're right, Lola!"

I'm happy until I remember what I'm about to forget—all my lines in *Once Upon a Pumpkin*. Fishsticks.

8. CUPCAKE QUEENS DON'T LIKE BEANS

"WE'RE THE CUPCAKE QUEENS,
we're the Cupcake Queens! We bring you fun!
And lots of frosting!" Amanda sings. She's good at
making up songs. But she didn't make that one up.
She got it right off the TV.

Amanda, Jessie, and Savannah are holding hands
and dancing in a circle.

"Cupcake Queens don't like beans!" I help out
Amanda from the outside of the circle. "They make
you toot. That's not for queens!"

Amanda stops singing. Jessie stops dancing. Savannah scowls at me. A scowl is a cross between *Scat!* and *growl*.

"Lola Zuckerman," Amanda says. "That is NOT a *Cupcake Queens* song."

"Cupcake Queens do not toot," Savannah says.

"It was your choice not to be a Cupcake Queen and take advantage of an absolutely free deluxe costume," Jessie informs me.

"That's because somebody—" I say.

"Is enjoying her brand-new puppy," Savannah interrupts.

Fishsticks.

"Besides, you're going to be a Zero and your mom will make you a really neat costume," Amanda says and pats me on the arm.

"Yay," I say and *yay* stands for *I changed my mind*. "But I have a different idea. I want to be a Cupcake Queen. Not Strawberry Sweetie Pie," I say before Savannah can open her trap. "Can't we make up a new one?"

"A new one?" Jessie says. "I don't get it."

"Like . . ." I think for a second. "Butterscotch Baby Cupcake Queen. I could be a little tiny baby Cupcake Queen."

"There's no such thing," Amanda says.

"That's not on the show," Jessie says. "That would be a spin-off show."

"That's four Cupcake Queens," Savannah says. "And there are only three."

Three Cupcake Queens. One Zero.

"Fine," I say. "I'm going to memorize my Pumpkin lines."

"Good idea," Jessie says. "'Cause you have the most lines in the play."

"How do you know?" I ask.

"Well, when my brother, Dustin, was in that play, he was the Pumpkin and he had to study all day and all night," Jessie says.

And now my tummy feels like I ate a pumpkin. A rotten one.

9. RUNAWAY DOG!

JACK LOOKS UP FROM HIS BOOK

100 Creepy TRUE Facts About Halloween. "So
you're the pumpkin in *Once Upon a Pumpkin*? I
was the moon. All I had to do was beam down on
the pumpkin patch and say, 'Don't worry, little
pumpkin!'"

I hang off my chair just like Harvey does. And
Once Upon a Pumpkin hangs with me. I have to
memorize SEVEN whole lines. That's TWO more
than anyone else.

"You better start learning your lines pronto," Jack says. "Before you know it—*BAM*—you're on that stage. The lights are shining on you. All those people are staring at you . . ."

I feel hot inside my eyeballs. And electricky. "STOP!" I yell.

Mom comes running in. She's got a big piece of green cloth on her shoulders and a measuring tape around her neck. She looks like Super Green Mom.

"Kids! Enough!" Mom says. She slaps two

spoons, some celery, and a jar of peanut butter on the table. "Two dresses down, twenty-eight to go," she mutters. Then she pauses and her eyes focus on me. "Lola, you absolutely, positively have to brush your hair after your bath tonight," she says.

"But—"

"No buts."

"Did you know people used to carve turnips, not pumpkins?" Jack tells us.

"Hmm," Mom says, and that stands for she wasn't even listening.

On the way out of the kitchen, she reaches into a cupboard and pulls out a box of raisins. "Catch!" she yells to Jack. And then she tosses the box of raisins to him. He catches it with one hand.

"Good throw, Mom," Jack yells. "Why are you wearing a cape?"

Mom smiles. "Like it?" Then she hurries back to the guest bedroom/sewing room.

"She didn't even make us our ants-on-a-log," I say.

"I guess we're big enough to make our own," Jack says.

"You are, but I'm not," I say. "And she forgot to ask me about my day." We look at the guest bedroom door, and guess what? It's shut tight like the lid on a pickle jar.

"Here," Jack says. He unscrews the peanut butter lid. He takes a scoop of peanut butter out and smears it all over the celery.

"That's not how you do it," I say. "Give me that." I take the peanut butter and spoon from him. "Watch

me." I carefully spoon peanut butter right down the celery aisle. Then I get out some raisins and plink them into the peanut butter. "See?" I hand one to him and then I make myself one. Patches whines for some peanut butter. He luh-huvs peanut butter.

I rest my feet on Patches. Poor Patches. "He's sad," I say. "He's starving to death."

"No, he's not," Jack says. "He already grabbed an apple off the counter."

"Oh. Well, he looks hungry."

Jack eats his ants-on-a-log in three bites. "Mm, that was good. Can you make me another one? I'll tell you more facts about Halloween."

I scoop more peanut butter and plink more raisins. Jack tells me that Americans spend six billion dollars on Halloween and eat ninety million pounds of chocolate. Then he wolfs down his ants-on-a-log.

But Jack's still hungry. We look in the fridge.

"There's baked macaroni and cheese in here,"

I say. "But I think it's for dinner." I hold up a big ol'
bag of mac and cheese that Mom made a hundred
years ago and froze and now it's thawing out.

"Maybe spoon me a few servings of that," Jack
says. "You're good at this, Lola. Here's another fact
for you. The signs of a werewolf are a unibrow, hairy
hands, and tattoos."

"But don't I have to heat it up or something?" I ask.

Jack looks at it.

"'Cause I'm not supposed to use the stove."

"Maybe we could ask Mom?"

Patches grabs the bag right out of my hand and takes off running.

"PATCHES!" I yell. "COME BACK HERE!"

Patches dives left into the living room.

"Kids, keep it down out there!" Mom warbles from the guest bedroom. "I'm trying to work in here."

Patches wings up the stairs. I race after him. Jack races after me.

"Jack, stay right there and catch him," I whisper-holler.

"No, you stay, and I'll chase him," Jack says. He sprints after Patches.

The front doorbell rings.

"Someone get the door!" Mom yells.

Jack and I freeze. Patches darts by with the mac and cheese bag hanging in his mouth. I grab it and—*zloop*. The bag slips right out of my hands. Patches goes bounding down the stairs with it.

"Bad dog!" I yell. But he rumbles like I gave him a compliment.

The doorbell rings again.

"COMING! I'm COMING," I hear Mom holler.

"PATCHES! What do you have in your mouth?"

I hurry down the stairs, zippety, zippety.

"Lola, you have some friends here," Mom calls. She's standing at the front door holding a slobbery bag of mac and cheese with teeth holes in it and cheese oozing out. She's got a piece of tape stuck right on her forehead. But I'm not about to tell her. No, sir. "We'll talk about how Patches got hold of the mac and cheese later, Lola," Mom loud-whispers. Then she says real sweet, "Come on in, girls."

Before we can even say a word, Mom hurries off. She calls, "Snacks in the kitchen," throws the drippy

bag of mac and cheese in the garbage, and then disappears into the guest room/sewing room.

It's Amanda, Jessie, and Savannah.

"We came to meet the puppy," Jessie tells me.

"You know," Savannah squeaks. "The PUPPY."

"The one you pinkie-promised about," Amanda says. She folds her arms up like a big ol' bandage.

Fishsticks.

10. ONCE UPON A WHOOOO

"WELL, WHERE IS IT?" JESSIE
asks.

Amanda is tap-tap-tapping her foot like a mad ol' woodpecker.

Savannah's face is red as the strawberry on Strawberry Sweetie Pie's head. "Amanda and Jessie wanted to come over to my house to see my puppy. I told them that my puppy missed its mom, so it had to go back to the Lola Puppy Farm. So you got a new puppy for me. Today. Right?"

"Riiiiight," I say.

"They wanted to see it. But we forgot to call you. So here we are!" Savannah says.

"We thought it was weird that the Puppy Farm is called the Lola Puppy Farm," Amanda informs me.

"Where's the puppy?" Jessie blares. "Here puppy, puppy, puppy!"

"Shush!" I say. "My mom has to make twenty-eight Lola dresses for the Kute Kids Clothing Company. Come on in, everybody," I whisper. I tiptoe into the kitchen. Patches trots right in. He wags his tail so hard his whole body wags.

"Well," Jessie says in her loud ol' TV voice. "There's Patches. Where's the puppy?"

Uh-oh.

Mom comes out of her guest room/sewing room. She has a pin in her mouth even though she told me to NEVER EVER do that.

"Girls, could you possibly take your play date outside?" Mom asks in her That's-Not-Really-A-Question Voice. "And Jack, why don't you go shoot some hoops?"

"Want me to teach you how to sink a ball blindfolded, Mom?" Jack asks.

"Maybe later," Mom says. "I've got to get back to work."

Jack slinks out the door.

I grab *Once Upon a Pumpkin* off the kitchen table.

"Let's go practice our lines. And when Mom's all done working, she can show us the puppy," I say.

"Great idea!" Savannah says.

"Why can't we see the puppy all on our own?" Jessie asks.

Amanda just folds up her arms and taps her foot. She hoists up one of her eyebrows and that means trouble.

"Because Mom said," I say. 'Cause it always shuts up me and Jack when Mom says that. Even if I need to explain that Jack told me it was okay to throw my mashed potatoes up to the ceiling to see if they would stick.

We go outside and flop in the grass and we let Patches sit with us even though he was a rascal.

"SCORE! I am awesome!" I hear Jack yell from the driveway.

"I'm a trick-or-treater," Jessie says.

"Me, too," Amanda adds.

"I'm the old lady," Savannah pipes up.

"I'm the pumpkin," I say.

Nobody says anything and that's what friends are for.

We all look at the play booklet. "You have the first line, Lola," Amanda says.

"'I'm just a lonely pumpkin, sitting in a pumpkin patch,'" I read out loud.

We all stare at the play booklet.

"Who's the black cat?" Amanda asks. "She has the next line."

"I think Madison," Jessie says.

"Can you just say it, Lola?"

"Then I might accidentally memorize it," I say. But I don't tell them I can barely keep the pumpkin lines in my head.

"Fine, I'll say it," Amanda says. "'Meow, meow, poor little pumpkin. You were too small to be chosen for a jack-o'-lantern.'"

We stop again.

"Who's the scarecrow?"

"I think Sam's the scarecrow," I say.

Amanda heaves out a big ol' sigh. "Fine. I'll be the scarecrow, too. 'Poor little pumpkin. You weren't ripe enough for pumpkin pie.' *PSSST*. Your turn, Lola."

"'And all the other pumpkins have been picked from the patch,'" I say in a really, really sad voice.

"'Tra-la-la, tra-la-la,'" Amanda sing-song says.

"'I'm just a trick-or-treater on my way to the pumpkin patch to pick the PERFECT PUMPKIN for Halloween.'"

"I'm tired of practicing," Jessie says. "I want to see an adorable, purebred puppy."

"Me, too," Amanda adds.

"Not me!" Savannah says. "I just love practicing for this play."

"Me, too!" I squawk like a big rooster.

Then even louder than me is another sound.

Whoooooooooooo. WHOOOOOOOOOOOOOOOO.

I scream, Amanda screams, and Jessie screams loudest of all.

10 ½. ONCE UPON A DWIGHT WHITE

"THERE IT GOES AGAIN!" JESSIE screams.

"IT'S THE GHOST!" I yell.

"It can't be a ghost," Savannah says.

"That has to be Jack," Amanda says, kind of trembly. "Right, Lola? He's just playing a trick on us."

"He's playing basketball," I say.

Suddenly, we hear the ghost again, only not so loud. *Whooo! Whooo!*

"It's coming from over there," I say and I point to the fence between our yard and Mrs. McCracken's. "Follow me."

"We're the Cupcake Queens," Savannah sings under her breath.

We creep like slugs over to the side of the house, to the fence.

I kneel down. Savannah kneels down. But Jessie and Amanda hang back and hold hands.

"*Howhoooooooo,*" the ghost howls.

"The ghost is visiting your neighbor," Jessie whispers.

"Maybe we should get my mom," I say.

Savannah shakes her head. "Remember Mrs. D.'s list?" she says. "Ghosts are make-believe, just like werewolves and zombies and—"

"*HOWHOOOOOOOOOOOOO . . .*" the ghost moans.

I take a peek through the space between the boards in the fence.

And guess what? You'll never guess. Not in a million years will you ever guess what I see.

"Ohhhhhh," I say.

Mrs. McCracken is standing on her back porch. Her pure-white kitty cat Dwight White is wrapped around her legs. Mrs. McCracken is singing, "The autumn winds are blowing. Bally hoo! Bally hoo! Whoo hoo hoo hoo!"

And Dwight White is yowling along with her.

"ROWR ROO! ROWR ROO!"

And guess what pops right out of my mouth? A laugh. A loud ol' laugh.

Mrs. McCracken drops her songbook and scoops up Dwight White. She marches across her yard and boy-oh-boy does she look mad. And mad on her looks like a red face and her nice shoes getting stuck in the mud so she's walking barefoot.

"Lola Zuckerman!" she yells. "Are you spying on me?"

"Nooo," I say as Dwight White leaps to the ground.

I forgot to say that Mrs. McCracken is always in a bad mood. That's 'cause she taught fifth grade for a hundred years.

"Say hi, everybody." Then I take a big step back so Amanda, Jessie, and Savannah can crowd up front.

"Hi, Mrs. McCracken," Amanda says. 'Cause she used to be Mrs. McCracken's neighbor, too. Before she moved to the boring part of town where you can't spy on your neighbors. "Hi, Dwight White," she says to Dwight White. He rides on Patches's back if Patches goes over there to dig.

I look over the top of Amanda's head so I can just barely see Mrs. McCracken's face, which looks a lot like a hot apple pie. She's kind of smiling, but then she stops up her smile.

"Well, Amanda Anderson, I'm disappointed to see you playing tricks on a poor old woman with your spying and screaming. I suppose Lola brought you into it."

"I did not!" I yelp.

"She did not!" Amanda says.

"We thought we heard a ghost," Jessie says. "It was moaning and screaming and howling."

Uh-oh. Mrs. McCracken's apple face turns straight into an eggplant and that's purple.

"Your cat is nice," Savannah says and she's crouching down and scratching Dwight White through the space between the fence boards.

But Mrs. McCracken doesn't care one bit, 'cause she reaches down and snatches up Dwight White.

"Very funny!" Mrs. McCracken hollers.

BAM! I hear our porch door slam shut. Mrs. McCracken is still yelling at me. "I may not be the world's greatest singer, but I certainly do NOT sound like a ghost."

"Hello, Mrs. McCracken," Mom warbles from the porch. "I hope the children aren't bothering you. Lola, Mrs. Anderson is here to pick up the girls!"

And that's what it means when Grampy Coogan says he's stuck between a rock and a hard place. Because I sure don't want to go inside. And I sure don't want to stay here with Mrs. McCracken and Dwight White.

Jessie takes off running right straight to Mom.

"Mrs. Zuckerman, can we please please please see your adorable new puppy that you got for Savannah?"

I run after Jessie and Amanda runs after me and

Savannah runs after Amanda and we all clump up around Mom.

"I'm not sure what puppy you're talking about," Mom says. "We don't have a puppy for Savannah." Mom gives me a look like she did the time I told her I was invited to live at the Andersons' house forever. "I'll tell Mrs. Anderson that you'll be right there."

"LOLA ZUCKERMAN!" Amanda yells as soon as Mom leaves. "I can't believe you pinkie-promised."

"You are really bad," Jessie says.

My insides squeeze so tight I can hardly breathe. "I'm sorry," I whisper, and it's not my voice saying that but my insides that can't breathe.

"GIRLS!" Mom hollers from far away.

"Well, why didn't you tell us she was lying?" Amanda asks Savannah.

Poor Savannah. Her face roses up. "I wanted to be a Cupcake Queen and Lola said if I didn't tell on her, she'd let me."

"That's not why," I say. "Well, not at first. I wanted you to be Strawberry Sweetie Pie Cupcake Queen 'cause you wanted to be."

Amanda folds her arms. Jessie growls, "Right."

11. UNDER NO CIRCUMSTANCES

FISHSTICKS.

Even though I wave and wave, Amanda won't wave back. I bet if I waved until my arm fell right out of the socket, Amanda wouldn't care. Jessie doesn't wave either. Savannah waves a little bit but then Jessie swats her arm down. 'Cause it wasn't her fault that I told a ball-face lie.

"Penny, as soon as I get this batch done, you and I have to get together," Mom says to Mrs. Anderson in the driveway.

"I would love that more than anything, Julie,"

Mrs. Anderson says. "And don't worry, hon! I've been busy, too."

"I'm excited to hear about your website business," Mom says.

Mrs. Anderson says, "Bye, now. And good luck finishing up the dresses."

While Mrs. Anderson gets into her car, Mom says to me, "I'll never for the life of me understand why Mrs. McCracken was singing in her backyard."

"Maybe she was singing to Dwight White," I say to Mom.

"She was NOT singing to Dwight White," Jessie says. *Bzzz.* Up goes the backseat window.

"Yes, she might have been!" I yell through the window. "My grampy has two dogs named Mr. and Mrs. Jones and he sings to them all the time."

Mrs. Anderson, Amanda, Jessie, and Savannah drive off.

Then Mom turns to me. "Why did you tell your friends that you had a puppy for Savannah?"

"I'm sorry, Mom," I say.

"I'm sorry, too," she says, and she takes my hand in hers.

"What am I going to do? Now Amanda, Jessie, and Savannah hate me."

Mom stares at something, and I think she didn't hear me. Then she says, "It's a problem, Lola. Lies do that. They make problems. So when you tell one, you have to figure out how to solve the problem."

Fishsticks. Mom went to Problem Solvers School, just like Mrs. D. and Principal McCoy.

12. DOWNER DINNER

FOR DINNER, MOM COOKS UP scrambled eggs on account of the baked mac and cheese being all slobbered on. Dad's in charge of the toast.

"Aw, scrambled eggs?" Jack says.

"Jack, that's one," Mom says with a bell inside her voice. On three we have to go to our rooms and that's a fact. We all take a helping of eggs.

"Take some vegetables and pass them on, Lola," Mom says.

I dig into the bag of baby carrots and pass them on to Jack.

"Since when does a bag of baby carrots count as vegetables?" Jack asks.

"That's two," Dad says.

"Not that I care. I don't even like vegetables."

I stare at Jack. Is he trying to get in trouble?

"Okay," I say, "Can I go first?" Every night we play a game where you say two things about your day. Everyone has to guess which one is true and which one is the lie.

"You went first yesterday, but fine," Jack says.

"Okay. Well . . . today I told Savannah Travers she could have my Cupcake Queen Halloween costume but I wish I hadn't said that—"

"Lola, I thought you wanted to be a zero!" Mom and Dad say at the same time.

"Because *zero* starts with *Z* and nobody appreciates zero," Mom adds.

"Well, I didn't think you had time to make me a costume this year," I say.

"Or me," Jack says.

"So how did it come about that you would be wearing a Cupcake Queen costume?" Mom asks.

"Well, Jessie's mom had three deluxe Cupcake Queen costumes that she got from the World's Deluxe Costumes catalog," I explain.

"And what about your mother who has been working hard to do her job *and* make you a wonderful zero costume?" Dad asks.

"You have?" I ask.

"How about me?" Jack asks in a voice that is eight sizes smaller than his regular voice. "Are you making me a Squad Frog costume for the sixth grade Monster Mash like you said you would?"

Mom puts down her forkful of eggs. She stands up and wraps Jack in a big ol' hug.

"You know I am," Mom says. And guess what, and you'll never guess so I'll just tell you.

Jack's eyes wet up. Then he smiles a big smile, so I might have imagined that.

"Both Zuckerman costumes are in progress," Mom says. "And will be better than anything you can buy in a catalog! Come see."

We follow Mom into the guest bedroom/sewing room, and wow—there's a Squad Frog green cape on the bed and green webbed feet. There's also a giant black-and-white striped zero.

"How did you make a perfect zero, Mom?"

"I sewed black and white cloth around a hula hoop!" she says.

RING! The doorbell buzzes.

"Now, who could that be?"
Mom asks.

I follow her to the door and
even from the window I can see
Savannah dressed as a Purple
Pony.

And she doesn't look happy.
Not one single bit.

● ● ●

When Mom opens the
door, Savannah Travers
is standing next to somebody who looks just like
Savannah Travers, only older. Purple Pony Savannah
is holding a deluxe Cupcake Queen costume in her
hand.

"I'm sorry to interrupt you during the dinner hour,"
the lady says. "I'm Paige Travers, Savannah's mom."

"I'm Julie Zuckerman," Mom says. "Lola's mom."

"And mine!" Jack hollers from the kitchen.

"Well, you see, Savannah's dad and I just learned how Savannah came to have this Halloween costume . . ."

"Why don't you come in?" Mom says. Mom ushers Mrs. Travers into our living room. Ushering is pushing with no hands. And our living room is where we go to have snacks before Thanksgiving. There's a chair in there that only Great-Aunt Sophie gets to sit on.

Mrs. Travers sits down on the fancy couch and says, "So Savannah has something she would like to say to Lola." Mom sits next to her. I sit next to Mom and Savannah sits next to me. It seems like we're on one of those talk shows Granny Coogan likes to watch when it's too rainy to garden.

Savannah says, "Lola, I'm sorry I made you feel bad so you decided not to be a Cupcake Queen. And then you couldn't be one 'cause I said I would tell on you about your lie. Here's your Cupcake

Queen costume back." Savannah puts the costume in my lap. It's itchy like Grandma's evening gowns.

"That's okay," I say really fast. "I don't even want to be a Cupcake Queen. Here," and I put it back on her lap.

Savannah's face perks up. Then she looks at her mom. Droop.

"That's very generous of you, Lola," Mrs. Travers says. "But Savannah can't accept this costume. Savannah, would you like to explain why?"

"Well . . ." Savannah says. "I used to watch *Purple*

Pony Pals and I really liked Priscilla Pony and my Aunt Kathy bought me a Priscilla Pony costume as a surprise even though she's a starving actress and doesn't have any money to waste."

"Well, I can't accept the costume either," I say. I know why I said that. But then I forget. So I swim around inside my head until I remember. Not lines I have to say in *Once Upon a Pumpkin* that are hard to remember. But what I'm feeling, 'cause that's easy to remember, 'cause I just felt it.

"I said I wanted to be a Zero because zero is last. But it could be the beginning. Like nobody knows how big a number might get when you add zeroes to the end. Also, my mom already started my costume."

I smile at Mom and she smiles at me. Then Mrs. Travers smiles at Mom and Mom smiles at her. It's like getting the giggles in class. Even if Mrs. D. told us to stop smiling, we'd have to keep on doing it.

My heart warms up like one of Grampy Coogan's

s'mores. "I wish that we could all live in my backyard. Patches and Amanda's dog, Barkley, and your cat, Arthur, and Jessie's designer dog. I wish nobody ever had to leave and go home."

"I bet when Patches does see Barkley, they're really happy!" Savannah says.

"Happier than just Barkley playing all the time with Jessie's dog that he probably gets tired of."

I think about that.

Then I give myself a big surprise. 'Cause I say, "But maybe sometimes Barkley likes playing with Jessie's dog. What's that dog's name, anyway?"

"Maizy."

"Oh. Maybe Maizy and Barkley and Patches could all have a dog playdate and play games you can't play with just two dogs. And maybe Arthur could come over and play, too."

Savannah smiles really, really big so that some of her freckles take a trip right across her cheek. "I would love that. But Arthur's kind of feisty, like Dwight White. Can I come over anyway?"

"Sure you can."

Our moms say goodbye, and I give Savannah a big surprise hug. A super-deluxe one that you can't get in a catalog.

12½. POOR PATCHES

"OH MY DURLING, OH MY durling, oooooh my durling Clementine, you are lost and gone forever, dreadful surry Clementine," I sing to Patches, Western-style. But no matter how much I sing, he just won't go to sleep.

He should be tired, because he helped me practice my lines over and over. AND he has to listen to me say them for ten more days.

"Come on, Patches," I say. We tiptoe down the hall and I hold on tight to Patches's collar. Me and

Patches don't believe in ghosts. But it's easier when you have a buddy.

I open Mom and Dad's door and creep in. *Tap, tap.* Mom leaps straight up.

"Lola, you scared the dickens out of me," Mom yowzas. Yowza is not a real word unless you know Grampy Coogan.

Dad snores away.

Mom takes a big breath. "Sweetheart, what's the matter?"

"Patches can't sleep," I explain.

"Oh, he can't? Well, maybe he belongs downstairs in his dog bed," Mom says. And right in the middle she yawns. A yawn is what you do when you're tired but you want to see what happens next.

"No, he doesn't," I say really fast. "'Cause he likes it better in my room."

"Well, not if he's keeping you awake," Mom says. She climbs out of her bed and puts on her robe and slippers because that's what oldish people do when they miss their cozy beds. Mom ushers me and Patches out of her room, down the hall, and back into my bed.

Mom tucks the covers up to my chin. "Why do you think Patches can't sleep?" she asks.

"He feels bad that he slobbered on the mac and cheese. And that he's always chasing Dwight White and causing a ruckus."

"Hmm. Yes. But then I think he feels sorry. And we forgive him, don't we, Lola?"

"But he can't say he feels sorry, Mom."

"No, but he shows it. And remember what Mrs. D. told you? Showing you're sorry is just as important as saying you're sorry."

"But Jessie and Amanda are so so mad at me, Mom," I say. And my voice goes this-a-way and that-a-way. "And maybe it was the final straw."

"Lola," Mom says, "I've known Amanda Anderson for a long time, and I believe she has a very big heart. And I've known you even longer, Lola dear. Your heart is just as big. When two friends have big hearts, they can get through a lot of problems."

"What about Jessie? Do you think she has a big heart?"

"Yes, I do think so."

Mom reaches down and kisses me on the
forehead and on each cheek.

"Goodnight, Lola. Tell Patches not to worry. We
love him and we forgive him."

13. DEAR JESSIE AND AMANDA

Dear Jessie,

    I'm really, really sorry for telling a whopper about Savannah's adorable cuddly brown dog, Jessie, with the big brown eyes and the wet pink tongue. I will try my best not to tell any more whoppers. And can I sometimes sit with Amanda on the bus and practice the Hand Jive? I can tell you all about the

Olden Days when me and Amanda
used to wear diapers.
    Love,
    Lola

P.S. I hope you like the four giant hearts
I drew. There's one for each of us.

Dear Amanda,

Do you remember that time when we were little? I mean that time when we decided to go on a walk and we only had on diapers? We ended up at Mrs. McCracken's house and she gave us animal crackers and apple juice? And when our moms came to get us, we didn't even want to leave. We were funny babies! We sure had a lot of adventures on Cherry Tree Lane.

I am sorry I fibbed about getting a puppy for Savannah. Especially since I pinkie-promised. That was a no-good dirty rotten thing and I bet you are thinking to yourself what is wrong with that Lola Zuckerman?

I tried to think about it and Mom helped me. I think I told you that whopper because I want you to like me best of all the people in the world. And the best people are the ones who get puppies for other people.

But Mom said only if you really do it. And somebody can still like you even if you don't get a puppy for them or even if they move away from your street.

My hand is all tired out from writing.

I hope you read my whole letter and your eyeballs didn't get tired out cause there's a surprise at the end.

I love you!

Sincerely,

Lola Katherine Zuckerman

P.S. I hope you like the four giant hearts I drew. There's one for each of us.

14. JUST A LONELY PUMPKIN

MY HEAD IS HAMMERING. THAT'S

because Mom combed my hair and OUCHY WA WA! That hurt, I'll tell you. My hair likes to knot up and that's not nice. From now on I'm going to brush my hair every single morning and every single night. Maybe.

And now Principal McCoy's banging on the microphone.

"Good afternoon, Cloverdale! We're excited to sponsor the 11th annual Cloverdale Second Grade

Play Festival. We think the kids are just as excited about performing their plays as they were about trick-or-treating last week."

"Wrong," Harvey whispers into my ear.

"First, we have a special treat from retired fifth grade teacher Mrs. Mary McCracken, who will be singing her original song, 'Dance of the Autumn Leaves.'"

Mrs. McCracken wobbles out onto the stage in her nice shoes that she must have cleaned the mud off of.

"Thank you, everyone," she says. And then she starts singing. The beginning part still sounds like a

ghost. But I'll never tell her that, 'cause I don't want to get her feeling all soupy again. And everyone has a right to yowl in their own backyard.

Right next to me Harvey is

hopping from one foot to the other.

I'm sweating inside my pumpkin costume that smells like Granny Coogan's attic. That's 'cause it gets handed down every autumn. But all the trick-or-treaters in the play get to wear their real costumes. So Amanda and Jessie are flouncing around in Cupcake Queens costumes. And even though they're talking to me again, it feels like winter inside my heart.

Finally Mrs. McCracken takes a bow. Everyone claps, including me. Mrs. McCracken comes bustling off the stage. Bustling is what you do when you're in a hurry but you're wearing a dress.

"You were good," I whisper really loud so Mrs. McCracken can hear.

"Thank you," Mrs. McCracken says but her face says *grrrrr*.

"And now it's time for *Once Upon a Pumpkin*, performed by Mrs. DeBenedetti's second-grade class," Principal McCoy says.

Harvey gives me a shove.

My legs are sweating and I can't make them move even though I tell them *Go!*

"I can't," I say. "I'm too scared."

"You have to," Harvey says. "You're the pumpkin."

I feel all bawly and not so good. I see Mrs. D.

from eight heads away. She has that smile on her face that says Oh Yes You Can.

All of a sudden there's a Cupcake Queen on one side of me. And a Cupcake Queen on the other side of me. And right in front of me there's an old lady.

"I'm sorry I lied about the puppy," I say in a dumb ol' blubber voice. "I only felt bad for Patches 'cause he's all on his own."

"No, he's not," Amanda says. "Barkley wants to play with him."

"Maizy wants to play with him too," Jessie says.

"And I want to watch," Savannah the old lady adds.

Principal McCoy taps the microphone. "And now we have *Once Upon a Pumpkin*."

"Okay," I say, and guess what? We have a pumpkin, cupcake, and old lady hug.

I roll out to the stage and I'm supposed to say something but I can't remember what it is. Not at all.

Then I remember how I felt.

And I say, "I'm just a lonely pumpkin, sitting in a pumpkin patch."

I smile big. So big. Because right over there I can see Amanda and Jessie and Savannah and they are my friends.

And we'll never fight again.

Maybe.

THE KIDS IN MRS. DEBENEDETTI'S SECOND GRADE CLASS (ALPHABETICAL ORDER)

Amanda Anderson

Harvey Baxter

Dilly Chang

Jessie Chavez

Abby Frank

Charlie Henderson

Sam Noonan

Sophie Nunez

Olivia O'Donnell

Madison Rogers

Rita Rohan

Ari Shapiro

Ruby Snow

Jamal Stevenson

Gwendolyn Swanson-Carmichael

John Carmine Tabanelli

Timo Toivonen

Savannah Travers

Ben Wexler

Lola Zuckerman

LOLA CALLS AMANDA

LOLA: Hi, Mrs. Anderson, this is Lola. Is Amanda there?

MRS. ANDERSON: Yes, Lola, just a minute, I'll get her. Oh, Lola, by the way, how is your mom doing?

LOLA: Good. She got her dress order done, and now she's soaking her hands in Jeri's All-Natural Cream.

MRS. ANDERSON: Oh, wonderful. Tell her I said hi.

LOLA: Okay, I will. Or you can. Want me to get her? MOM!!!!!! It's Mrs. Anderson on the phone even though I called Amanda.

MOM (FROM A DISTANCE): OH, LOLA, PLEASE TELL PENNY I'LL CALL HER BACK.

LOLA: Sorry, Mrs. Anderson. Her hands are still soaking.

MRS. ANDERSON: That's fine. Here's Amanda.

LOLA: Hi, Amanda! It's me, Lola. Lola Zuckerman.

AMANDA: I know it's you, Lola. And you don't have to say Zuckerman! You're the only Lola I know!

LOLA: You're the only Amanda I know, but not the only Anderson.

AMANDA: What other Anderson do you know?

LOLA: Carolyn Peterson-Anderson.

AMANDA: Peterson-Anderson isn't the same thing as Anderson.

153

LOLA: Okay.

AMANDA: She's in kindergarten.

LOLA: 'Member when we were in kindergarten?

AMANDA: I wore a new purple skirt on the first day. And you accidentally wrote on it during art.

LOLA: Oh, yeah. I caught a grasshopper at the bus stop.

AMANDA: Mr. Bell helped you find a new habitat for it at recess. And you picked me for a helper. Only I was scared of the grasshopper's twitchy legs, so I cried.

LOLA: 'Member the Kindergarten Halloween Parade?

AMANDA: Yes. You were right behind me. You stepped on my Glitter Princess costume and got a footprint on it.

LOLA: And it kind of came off.

AMANDA: Lola, why did you call me?

LOLA: I called to see if you could come over to play. But you probably don't want to.

AMANDA: Why don't I want to?

LOLA: 'Cause.

AMANDA: Lola, remember when I threw up on my desk?

LOLA: Oh, yeah. Gwendolyn Swanson-Carmichael screamed.

AMANDA: And Harvey called me Barf Baby.

LOLA: I didn't get in trouble for hollering at him.

AMANDA: And we waited for my mom in the nurse's office.

LOLA: We cuddled like sick baby bunnies lost in the forest.

AMANDA: Only we were in the nurse's office.

LOLA: Then you went home and our whole class made you get-well cards.

AMANDA: Then you threw up on the bus.

LOLA: And the whole class made me get-well cards, too.

AMANDA: I liked yours best.

LOLA: I liked yours best, too.

AMANDA: Mom says I can come over. But did you check with your mom?

LOLA: Yes, I did. Definitely.

AMANDA: Pinkie promise over the phone?

LOLA: Just a minute. MOM? CAN AMANDA COME OVER?

MOM: YES!

LOLA: Pinkie promise.

SNEAK PREVIEW OF

Last-But-Not-Least

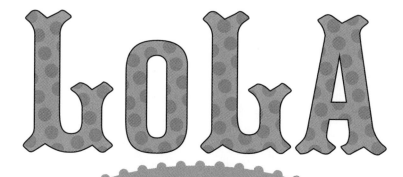

LOLA

AND A KNOT
THE SIZE OF TEXAS

BOOK FOUR

1. HUSH ABOUT THE BRIGHT BLUE BRUSH

MY NAME IS LOLA ZUCKERMAN, and Zuckerman means I'm always last. Just like zippers, zoom, and zebras. Last. Zilch, zeroes, and zombies.

ZZZZZZZ when you're too tired to stay awake. *ZZZZZZZZ* when a bee is about to sting you. *Z*. Ding-dong LAST in the alphabet.

"FOR THE LOVE OF PETE!" I yell.

"Lola, don't cuss on the bus!" Amanda says. "Now, HOLD STILL, I told you."

"Yeah, Lola, hold still," Jessie says. "You've got the WORST hair knot I've ever seen."

I hold still, all right. If I don't, Amanda Anderson might just pull all the hair right out of my head.

"I . . . almost . . . almost . . . almost—"

"YOWCH!" I yell. "Stop that, Amanda!" I smooth

down the big hair knot on the back of my head. "That's good enough."

"Nuh-uh," Amanda says. "It's stuck in there. Your mom will get it out for you, I bet."

"No, sir," I say. "Right before the second grade play she almost killed my whole head." Mom has a bright blue brush that can make curly hair straight. It can turn a poodle into a collie. That bright blue brush and I are best enemies.

"Amanda, what did your mom say about adopting cats?" Jessie asks. She turns to me. "Amanda wants to adopt brand-new deluxe rescue cats."

"I know that," I say. "Remember? Amanda told us last week at our Morning Meeting." I think about fibbing that we're getting some rescue cats, too. And a rescue guinea pig and a rescue horse. Plus some rescue chickens. But I still remember fibbing about getting Savannah Travers a brand-new puppy. So I keep my trap shut.

Except I ask: "Did your mom say yes?"

"She said no," Amanda says.

Sal pulls our bus up to Amanda and Jessie's stop.

Amanda's mom and Jessie's grandma are waiting. Mrs. Anderson has a hold of Barkley, and Jessie's grandma has Maizy, Jessie's purebred West Highland Terrier. I have a burp in my heart 'cause I feel bad that Patches is the only dog at our bus stop. He's all by his lonesome self.

"BYE, AMANDA!" I yell before she climbs off the bus.

"Bye, Lola," she says.

"Bye, Jessie," I say.

Pretty soon it's my stop.

"*Adiós, amiga,*" Sal calls.

Mom waves to Sal. She's in her car at the bus stop. Shucks. That means errands.

I stomp over to Mom's car and knock on her window. *RRRR.* Down it goes.

"Get in, Lola Lou," Mom says.

"Why is Jack in the front seat?"

Jack leans forward and gives me a Jack-o-Lantern smile. "Because I'm a big kid."

"Remember, Lola?" Mom asks.

I'm not tall enough for the front seat, even though I stretch myself every night. I climb into the backseat right next to a big bolt of fabric and buckle myself up. "Where are we going?"

"Shopping."

I groan. "For clothes?" All those itchy tags and sales ladies—*blech*! I don't like shopping for clothes. No, sir.

Mom says. "No, food shopping. And I have a surprise."

"What-what-what?" I ask.

"I was going to wait to tell you, but Granny thought . . . ," Mom says.

Jack answers, "Granny and Grampy Coogan are coming for Thanksgiving. When they went home this summer and you bawled your eyes out . . ."

"I did not!"

"They bought tickets and kept it a big surprise," Jack informs me.

"Then how do you know?" I ask Jack.

He just shrugs. "I'm older. I know stuff."

"They thought we would *all* enjoy their company," Mom says.

I forget about mad. "They're coming?" I hop up and down in my seat.

"In three days," Mom says.

"Grandma's still coming, too? Right, Mom?"

"That's right," Mom says.

"Are we having olives?" Jack says. "I'm going to put one olive on every finger and eat them off."

"Me, too!" I hop up and down, up and down, like I do on Jack's pogo stick when he says I can use it.

Then my hop stops.

I think of something bad about having ALL those grandparents at Thanksgiving.

My grandmas ALWAYS ask me and Jack TWO HORRIBLE QUESTIONS. "How do you like my pumpkin pie? Is it the best pumpkin pie you ever tasted?"

It's like being the rope in a tug-of-war game.

Jack told me to tell BOTH of them their pie is the best. I know that's lying. I know one is better.

I know one tastes like licking a candle. I'm not telling which. So I lie to one of those grannies. Now both grannies are going to be in one place. My house. What if they find out I'm lying? What if I get caught?

Lying is bad. And so is getting caught.

OCT - - 2017